This Book Belongs to:

....

With special thanks to Valerie Wilding
To Niamh Allan

EGMONT

We bring stories to life

Magic Farm: Friends Forever
First published in Great Britain 2011
by Egmont UK Limited
239 Kensington High Street
London W8 6SA

ISBN 978 1 4052 5529 5

1 3 5 7 9 10 8 6 4 2

www.egmont.co.uk

A CIP catalogue record for this title is available from the British Library

Printed and bound in Great Britain by the CPI Group

CONTENTS

A Secret Fear

'Hi, Aidan, I'm just coming,' Olly Thompson yelled out to his friend. 'I have to wash my wellies first. If they get any muddier, I'll be a walking, talking Mud Monster.'

Aidan sat on the gate, swinging his long legs. 'Get a move on, Olly. Hannah's lesson is nearly finished – you don't want to miss yours.'

That's exactly what I do *want*, Olly thought. The Thompsons – Olly, his sister Hannah and their mum and dad – had moved to Golden Valley Farm recently. Olly loved everything about farm life, except the idea of ever riding a pony. He liked baby foals – they were small and cute – but secretly, he was scared of bigger ponies and horses. Today, Aidan's aunt Molly was giving Hannah her first riding lesson on their new pony, Toffee. Olly was meant to go after Hannah, but he was hoping Aunt

Molly would run out of time.

He scraped off the last of the mud and shoved his feet into the wellies.

'Come on, slow coach!' Aidan called, racing ahead.

With a heavy heart, Olly trudged after him. Outside, Max, the Thompson family's sheepdog, ran in excited circles. Over in the paddock, Olly saw Hannah sitting up straight in the saddle.

Aunt Molly called to her. 'Keep your knees close to the saddle – *good girl*! Heels down, Hannah, toes in. Excellent!'

Aidan glanced at Olly. Olly tried to grin at his friend, but it was hard to smile when he felt so uncertain.

'You OK?' Aidan asked.

Olly nodded. 'I was just thinking there's an awful lot to learn.'

'Aunt Molly's a great teacher, so don't worry about that.'

They watched her show Hannah how to dismount. The two of them fussed over Toffee, telling her what a good pony she was.

When Hannah brought Toffee over, Max's tail went into a spin. He loved the other farm animals.

'That was such fun!' said Hannah, her face shining. 'I can't wait for my next lesson.'

'All farm people should learn to ride,' said Aidan.

'Why?' said Olly. 'Farmers have

tractors and trucks. Why do they

need horses?'

Aidan shrugged. 'Can't think of a

more fun way to get around the farm,

can you?'

'I can't,' said Hannah. 'Aidan,

I bet you could ride before you

could walk.' She smiled fondly at

Toffee. 'How could anyone not want

to ride our lovely little pony!'

Little? thought Olly. That saddle looked a long way off the ground.

Aunt Molly called across the paddock. 'Olly, you're a bit late but don't worry, I've got just enough time to teach you how to mount Toffee before we take her saddle off.'

Olly thought quickly. What reason

could he give Aidan's aunt for not wanting to ride?

'Er, I've got a bit of stitch, actually,' he said, clutching his sides. 'I think I ate too much breakfast.'

Aunt Molly shook her head. 'We don't want you getting in the saddle if you're in pain. Same time tomorrow?'

'Er . . .' Olly was saved by Max,
who dropped a rubber bone at Aunt
Molly's feet. She picked it up and
threw it for him, laughing as she

watched Max race after it.

'Silly dog,' she muttered, walking after him.

Phew, Olly thought. But Aidan was chatting away about how they could go riding together soon. Olly stared hard at the ground, willing his friend to stop. He could feel his cheeks colouring. When he glanced back up,

Aidan had stopped talking, and was looking at him oddly.

Olly's heart sank. *Aidan's guessed*, he thought. *Now he'll tease me about being frightened.*

But Aidan didn't make fun of him. 'Aunt Molly won't make you do anything scary,' he said. 'You don't need to be afraid.'

Olly nodded, biting his lip.

'You live on a farm now, Olly,' Aidan said. 'You'll need to learn to like *all* the animals.'

Even though Olly knew his friend was being kind, he was embarrassed. Then he had an idea. He knew just the thing to make Aidan and Hannah forget about horse riding!

'Hannah'll be finished at the stable soon,' he said. 'Let's do something exciting. Let's go to Magic Farm!'

Aidan's eyes gleamed. 'Oh yeah! The Hayseeds are sure to be up to something fun.'

The Hayseeds were scarecrows who lived in a very special place called Magic Farm. Only Olly, Hannah and

Aidan knew the secret way to get there. And the Hayseeds weren't just ordinary scarecrows . . . they walked, and talked, and laughed and everything!

'Hannah!' Olly called as his sister emerged from the stable. 'Magic Farm?'

'My first riding lesson *and* a visit

to Magic Farm, all in one day,' she cried. 'Brilliant! Well, what are we waiting for?'

Rain, Rain, Go Away!

Olly flew up the hill behind Golden Valley Farm, beating Aidan and Hannah to the top.

'What did you have for breakfast, Olly?' said Aidan. 'Runner beans?'

Olly grinned. He paused to look at the scarecrow that stood a little way down the other side of the hill, one of its arms outstretched. Mist swirled below it. Olly's heart was beating fast. This scarecrow was the key to their secret!

'To the scarecrow!' Olly cried. 'One . . . two . . . three . . . GO!'

Aidan's long legs took him down faster than the others. Olly and Hannah were neck and neck, but Olly slowed down to watch Aidan grab hold of the scarecrow's arm and run round it. No matter how many times Olly saw this happen, it still amazed him. One moment Aidan was there, the next – he had vanished!

'Now me.' Hannah held the scarecrow's hand and walked round, nose in the air, as if she was doing a fancy dance.

Olly drew a sharp breath as his sister disappeared. His turn now! He held the scarecrow's arm, feeling the stuffing scrunch beneath his fingers. Round he went. *Whoosh*. Everything whizzed into a silvery blur. After a moment's silence he was flung forwards, but he pulled himself upright before bumping straight into

Hannah and Aidan.

'Whoa!' Olly said. 'What a way to travel!' The landscape had changed and now he could see Magic Farm, with its pretty farmhouse covered in scarlet creeper. As always, pale pink, blue and gold clouds bobbed over it. But today big, silvery-grey ones took up most of the sky. And something else was different. 'The sun has lost its sparkle,' Olly said, frowning.

The sun over Magic Farm usually sent out sparkles of light. Now, the grey clouds hid it.

'Ha-ha-hat-tishoo!'

A hat flew up from behind a bush.

Olly grinned. 'Is that Tishoo?'

Aidan laughed. 'It must be. His hat

always leaps off his head whenever he sneezes!'

Hannah crept closer to the bush to take a peek. The leaves rustled, as if something big was disturbing them. Then two scarecrows burst out, their stitched mouths gaping in fear. One wore torn, untidy clothes and had a grubby face. The other looked a little smarter: his jacket still had buttons and he wore a slightly squashed hat. Bits of straw poked from their sleeves. Both scarecrows were clutching brooms, but they lowered them when they saw the children.

'Muck, Tishoo,' said Olly. 'Hi!'

'Hello! Ha-ha-hat-tishoo!' Tishoo caught his hat before it sailed away.

Muck tried hurriedly to explain what was going on. 'They scared Star . . . threw mud at her . . . must find them . . . chase them away . . .'

Muck wasn't making much sense, but the children knew enough about Magic Farm to understand. Muck was trying to tell them that the Little Rotters – the naughty creatures who were always trying to mess things up for the Hayseeds – were causing trouble yet again.

Olly took Muck's broom. 'It's really brave of you to look for the Little Rotters.' He knew all the Hayseeds were very scared of the mischievous creatures. 'Would you like us to help you find them?'

'And can you help us chase them away too?' Muck asked.

Hannah patted his arm. 'Of course we can.'

Aidan took Tishoo's broom and he and Olly swished under the bushes. Suddenly, Olly spotted something orange moving behind one of them. Hannah pointed and shrieked a loud warning: 'Rotter!'

Olly darted round the bush. He was surprised to find a small orange-and-pink spotty squirrel glaring at him. 'Sorry, little one,' he said, and went back to the others.

The squirrel followed, chattering crossly. 'Gak! Gak!'

With a flick of its bushy tail, the squirrel ran up Tishoo's leg, kept on climbing, and settled on his head.

Tishoo sneezed. 'Ha-ha-hat-tishoo!' and the squirrel jumped down in alarm.

Olly laughed. 'Your hat stayed on for once, Tishoo!'

Aidan popped up from the middle

of a bush with a blue-and-white striped field mouse perched on his shoulder.

It wiggled its nose and leapt away. 'Where are the other Hayseeds?' he asked.

'Sunny and Patch are in the stable, grooming mud off our friend, Star,'

Muck explained. 'She's the one the Little Rotters frightened.'

What type of friend needed grooming? Olly wondered, going to look behind another bush.

'Poor Star,' said Tishoo. 'We want her to be happy.'

'Yes, and we need her to help us with the planting,' Muck added.

Olly backed out of a tangly bush. 'Why not use the Duzzit to do the planting?' He knew Magic Farm's special machine could do practically any farm job.

'The Duzzit's busy,' said Muck. 'The bluecurrants all decided to ripen at once. We can't pick them, because the trees they grow on are too high.

So the Duzzit is doing it.'

'Why are you in such a hurry to do the planting?' asked Olly.

Muck pointed to the silver clouds. They barged across the sky, bumping the little fluffy ones out of the way. 'Rain's coming,' he said. 'It'll be like a waterfall, on and off, for days. We won't be able to plant then.'

'Let's go to the farmyard in case it starts soon,' said Hannah.

Aidan gathered the brooms. 'You just want to see Star,' he teased.

Hannah laughed. 'So what! I want to see who this new friend is. I bet it's a pony.' They set off with Muck and Tishoo.

Olly followed slowly. Just as

they neared the white picket fence that surrounded the yard, Muck squealed.

Peeping through the gate were two grinning faces topped with bright orange hair.

Little Rotters!

A Ticklish Problem

The Little Rotters scrambled over

the gate and landed . . . *SPLASH!* . . .

in a large silvery puddle. Shrieking,

'Muddy puddy! Muddy puddy!' they

scooped handfuls of mud and flung

it at Hannah and Muck, who were

nearest.

'I'll get them!' said Aidan crossly

as they raced away, giggling.

Olly stopped him. 'They've had their fun,' he said. 'Maybe now they'll leave the Hayseeds alone for a bit.'

'Come and meet Star,' Muck said, leading them into the stable.

Sunny was so happy to see the children again that she couldn't stop dancing. Patch patted their backs, saying, 'Good to see you!

Glad you came! Glad you came!'

'We found some Little Rotters by the gate,' Muck told them, 'but they ran away.'

'After they splashed us with mud,' said Hannah. 'Now I know how poor Star got messy . . .' Her voice trailed away. Olly came to stand beside her and the two of them stared, open-mouthed, at the most beautiful farm animal they'd ever seen. Star wasn't a pony, or even a stallion – she was a zebra, with a glittering black mane and a bright silver star right in the centre of her forehead.

'She's amazing,' Hannah breathed, drawing nearer to stroke the zebra's nose. Between blotches of dried mud,

Star's coat had thick stripes of black and white.

'Where did she come from?' Olly asked, staying well back. They'd never seen an animal like this on Magic Farm before.

'There were some shooting stars last night,' one of the scarecrows explained, smiling. 'One of the stars landed in the farmyard, and when we went to investigate, Star was waiting for us. She's a beauty, isn't she? We're sure she's been sent to help with the planting.'

'She certainly is beautiful,' Aidan murmured.

Sunny swept a brush gently across Star's coat, over and over, removing a

little more mud each time.

Star tossed her head and swished her tail. Suddenly, she stamped and shuffled away from Sunny.

'Star doesn't want to be groomed,' Sunny sighed. 'But I'm being gentle.'

'Perhaps the brush is rough,' Hannah suggested.

'I don't think so.' Sunny passed it

to Hannah. 'Feel it. Have a go.'

Hannah ran the bristles across her hand. 'It feels fine,' she said, and began to brush.

Olly was sure Star would settle now. Animals always loved Hannah. But after just two sweeps of the brush, Star became jumpy again. It made Olly a bit nervous.

Patch peered outside. 'The clouds are building,' he said. 'We *must* get her clean and start planting before the rain starts.'

Hannah looked interested. 'If Star's going out to work, why not clean her afterwards to save doing it twice?'

Patch beckoned them over to the doorway. 'See that planter?'

He pointed to a long, low wooden machine, with a bucket on top and a thick slab of wood at the back, like a shovel. At the front was a pole with a pointed lower end.

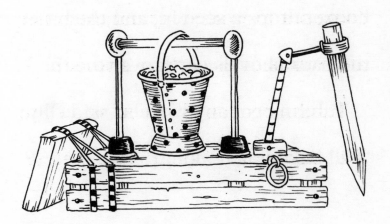

'I've never seen a thing like that before,' said Aidan.

'That's a Magic Farm machine,' Muck explained proudly. 'The pole punches a hole in the ground, the bucket drops a seed in, and the bit at the back shovels earth over the top.'

'It hasn't got any wheels,' said Olly. 'Will Star drag it along?'

'You'll see!' said Patch.

'But I still don't understand why you can't groom Star *after* planting,' Hannah said.

'I know why,' said Aidan. 'The planter will be harnessed to Star, and it will rub her muddy coat and make her sore.'

Sunny smiled. 'You *are* clever!'

Aidan looked pleased with himself.
'Shall I groom Star?' he asked. 'Zebras
are a bit like horses, and I can handle
those.'

Hannah handed Aidan the brush,
but when he put it against Star's
tummy, she shuffled away again with
a whinny.

Olly had an idea. He thought the

others might laugh at it, but they had to try something. 'When I was little,' he said, 'and Mum bathed me, I always tried to wriggle away when she washed under my arms.'

'That's because you're ticklish,' said Hannah.

Patch frowned. 'You mean Star might be . . .'

Olly nodded. 'Maybe she's ticklish too. Perhaps you need to be extra careful when you're brushing her sides.'

'Good thought, Olly,' Aidan said. 'Here, take the brush. Show us where we have to be careful.'

Olly didn't move. He didn't want to get too close to Star.

'Go on,' Aidan said quietly. 'I'll stand beside you.'

Slowly, Olly moved nearer to Star. Very gently, he ran his hand down one of the stripes on her side, and followed it with a firm sweep of the brush. She didn't jump!

Olly brushed again and again. Each time, he ran his hand over Star's side

first and followed it with the brush.

Each time, more mud came away.

He found himself talking softly to the

zebra.

'A little lower now, Olly,' Sunny

told him.

Olly forgot his nerves, even when

Star nuzzled him with her nose.

'Star's so relaxed, her eyes keep

closing!' Sunny said. 'You've made a friend for life, Olly.'

He felt himself turn pink with pleasure.

When Star was ready, Aidan whispered, 'Well done, Olly. You have the magic touch.'

Olly didn't think he could feel any happier.

Olly in Charge

Star clopped to the field, where Patch put her harness on and fastened a polished leather strap under her tummy. 'Her coat's gleaming almost as much as the star on her forehead,' he said. 'Thank you, Olly.'

Olly watched Patch buckle the planter to straps at the side, so Star could pull it. 'I'll help the other Hayseeds watch for Little Rotters,' he said.

But Patch stopped him. 'Star seems to trust you, Olly. Would you like to walk beside her, and keep her moving

in a nice straight line?'

Olly paused, then patted Star gently

and took the rein. 'Sure,' he said.

He smiled to himself. *If Patch had*

asked me that an hour ago, I would have been afraid! he thought. *But Star and I are friends now.*

'Come on, girl.' He hoped the planter wasn't too heavy for Star. It seemed silly not to put wheels on it. But Star picked up speed, and when Olly glanced behind to make sure the planter was running straight, he nearly fell over in surprise. 'It's got legs!' he said.

The planter had eight little legs, four on each side, with funny wooden feet. Round and round they went, helping the planter move along. And it wasn't just any old seeds that were being dropped into the ground. As Olly watched over his shoulder, magical sweet surprises fell into the earth. A red-and-white striped candy cane slid into one hole and, in the next second, up popped a whole bush with candy canes dangling from its branches. Then some candy floss floated down and a mass of quivering pink candy-floss fruit began to grow from the ground. Next came a row of brightly coloured swirly lollipops!

'We're growing sweets!' Olly called to the others.

'Not just any type of sweets!' one of the scarecrows called back. 'These ones won't rot your teeth!'

Olly carried on walking with Star. He loved it when she turned her head and nuzzled his shoulder.

76

71

Back and forth they went, making holes, dropping flying saucers and chocolate balls and marshmallows. Piles of sweets grew from the ground. But all the time, heavy silver clouds were gathering.

Hannah and Aidan leant over the field gate. 'You're doing really well,' Aidan shouted.

The Hayseeds were gazing up at the clouds, looking worried.

'Come on, Star,' said Olly, 'one more length of the field and we're done.'

The zebra whinnied, as if to say, 'Hooray!'

They'd almost planted the last row when there was a sudden snap and Star stopped. Olly looked to see what was wrong. 'A buckle's broken on the planter,' he said. 'Hey, Patch! We need help.'

Everyone hurried across the field.

'I can fix that,' said Aidan, but Sunny shook her head.

'Let's unhitch Star,' she said. 'The planting's nearly done anyway and we should get her inside before the rain starts.' As Sunny undid the other buckle, Star started stamping and tossing her sparkly mane.

'Quiet, girl.' Olly gently stroked her, but even he couldn't calm her. What was spooking Star? He glanced around and saw a flash of orange through the hedge. Then he heard high-pitched giggling, and three mischievous little faces

peeped out.

'Oh no! Little Rotters!'

Olly gasped. 'They're laughing

at us because the planter's broken.'

The Hayseeds ran, squealing, in

all different directions. Aidan and

Hannah shouted, 'Go away!' but

the Little Rotters just ran gleefully

after the terrified scarecrows.

'We'll take care of the Hayseeds,' Hannah shouted to Olly. 'You look after Star!'

Now more Little Rotters squeezed through the hedge and shouted and waved in front of the zebra.

Star jolted backwards, then she turned and galloped off, chased by

the Little Rotters. She sped through an open gate into a meadow that led to a wide stream. But just then, the Little Rotters spotted a short cut through the hedge.

Olly wriggled through after them. 'Leave Star alone!' he yelled.

The Little Rotters giggled as they scampered after the zebra. Behind him, Olly heard Aidan and Hannah calling out support.

'You can catch Star, Olly. We know you can!' called Hannah.

'Star trusts you,' added Aidan.

Olly knew Star was afraid of the Little Rotters. She'd never come back until they'd gone. He had to get rid of them. But how?

Clever Star

Star galloped across the meadow towards the stream. It was too wide to jump, so the poor zebra went round in circles, her stripes blurring. She was trying to stay far away from the

Little Rotters, but they were getting closer. Olly had to distract them!

He spotted a nearby tree. *That's it. A climbing competition!* The tree's lowest branch was quite high up. Olly wasn't sure he could make it. He ran, thrust a foot against the trunk and sprang as high as he could. Yes! He grasped the branch, the tree bark rough against his hands. Swinging his feet towards the tree trunk, he climbed. His muscles strained as he pulled himself up on to the branch, then he sat for a moment, taking in deep breaths.

'Oi!' he shouted, climbing on to the next branch. 'Little Rotters! Bet you can't climb as high as me!'

The Rotters stopped.

Olly hoped they would come after him. *Then they'll leave Star alone,* he thought.

'Hey! I'm the best climber ever!' he yelled. 'Better than you. An *ant* could climb a tree faster than a Little Rotter!'

That did it. The Little Rotters ran

towards him and threw themselves at the tree trunk. Their small hands found holds in the knobbly tree bark. Looking down, he saw a ring of grinning faces as they all started to climb up to him.

Where's Star?

Olly looked across the meadow and was relieved to see her standing

86

further down the stream, calmer now
that she wasn't being chased.

The Rotters hadn't got far up the
trunk. They began grumbling.

'Stupid tree.'

'Nasty knobbles.'

One of them squealed angrily,
jumped down and pointed to Star.
'More fun!' he cried, and they all set

off again to chase the zebra.

'Oi oi!' someone shouted.

'Get *away*!' yelled another voice.

Olly breathed a sigh of relief as he spotted Hannah and Aidan, waving brooms around. They circled the Little Rotters.

'To the stream, over there!' cried Aidan pointing up the bank, away from where Star was standing.

'But they'll sink in the water!' Olly called over. Even though they didn't like Little Rotters, he didn't want them to get hurt.

'Oh don't worry,' replied Hannah, sweeping a Little Rotter towards the bank. 'The Hayseeds say they float like corks. They hate water because

it makes them clean!'

The Little Rotters toppled into the stream and Star cantered away. From his perch in the tree, Olly could hear the Rotters yelling rude remarks.

'Nasty childrens!'

'Hopes you fall over!'

Some of them scrambled up on to the far bank, shaking fists. At least they were out of the way. Hannah and Aidan hurried to the tree.

'Climb down, Olly,' said Aidan. He looked over his shoulder at Star, who was pressing herself nervously against a fence. 'She'll feel safe again if she sees you.'

Olly clambered down to the low branch then realised, with a sinking feeling, that he was stuck. 'I can't. It's too far. If I jump from here I could sprain my ankle.'

'How did you get up there in the first place?' Hannah asked. 'I doubt if Aidan could have done it, even with his long legs.'

Olly shrugged. 'I was just desperate to help Star, and –'

'And you used your super powers!' laughed Aidan. 'Don't worry. We'll fetch a ladder.' They hurried off.

Olly settled down to wait, keeping an eye on Star. After a few moments she walked towards him, coming to a standstill beneath his branch. Her broad back gleamed below him.

'Hello, girl,' he murmured.

She stood quietly.

Olly realised what was happening.

'You want to help me, don't you?'

Star whinnied softly.

If I hold this branch tightly, he

thought, *maybe I could swing myself down on to Star's back*. But did he dare? What if she moved?

He made up his mind. Star trusted *him*, so he should trust *her*. He talked to her softly as he got ready. She stayed perfectly still.

Here goes, he thought. Gripping the branch firmly, he dropped his legs and swung them out. But he only kicked empty air. He couldn't reach Star! *Closer, come closer*, he begged her silently.

Star edged nearer. Was it enough? Or would he end up sprawled on the ground with a sprained ankle?

Olly took a deep breath and let go. 'Whooooa!' he yelled, twisting as he fell through the air.

Rainbow's End

'Ooof!' He'd landed safely. He was on horseback . . . or *zebra* back! And no saddle, either. The ground was a long way down, but Olly was sure Star would be steady for him.

He patted Star's neck. 'We did it!' he said. 'What a team!'

Olly didn't know how to make Star walk, but he didn't need to worry. She set off across the meadow and he felt quite safe, gently holding her twinkling mane for balance as he watched her head bobbing in time to each step.

The sun went in as a great silver cloud bounced a little pink puffball aside. Olly realised he'd forgotten about the coming rain.

He heard a shout and looked up. Hannah, Aidan and the Hayseeds were marching to him, holding a ladder over their heads. Olly laughed. 'You look like a giant centipede!'

Hannah ducked out from beneath the ladder. 'We came to rescue you,' she said.

Olly grinned. 'Too late. Star got there first.'

Aidan said, 'About . . . turn!'

They all shuffled round to face the other way. With Olly and Star in the lead, they made their way across

the field, avoiding the newly planted sweets. Even Star walked carefully. *Just as if she doesn't want to spoil her hard work*, thought Olly.

As they reached the farmyard, a large silvery cloud drifted above them, stopped, and released millions of glittering raindrops. Everyone got wet!

'A nice shower for the new seeds!'

called Olly, watching silver drops mix with the sparkles of Star's mane.

Outside the stable, Star stopped next to a platform so Olly could slide off her. Then they hurried inside after the others. Patch found a pile of old red towels and passed them round. When Hannah began to rub her hair dry, Olly couldn't believe his eyes –

as the towel got wet, it turned from red to silver!

He used his towel to rub Star down, before wiping his own dripping face.

Aidan nudged him and said, 'Hey, you're putting Star first. That's just what a real horseman would do.'

Olly grinned happily.

'A big thank you to Hannah, Aidan and Olly,' Muck declared, 'for helping us plant the sweets before the rain came.'

'And for getting rid of those nasty Little Rotters again!' added Sunny.

'Thank Star too,' said Olly. 'She worked really hard.'

'Hooray for Star!' They all cheered

softly, trying not to startle the zebra.

Aidan grinned. 'I don't think Star would care if we cheered at the tops of our voices,' he said. 'That's because you're here, Olly. She really trusts you.'

Olly nodded. 'I trust her, too.'

Hannah looked outside. 'The rain's almost stopped,' she announced.

'The sun's sparkling again.'

Everyone went outside – even Star. The sun sent sparkles across the sky and, as they twinkled through the raindrops, a rainbow appeared.

Hannah stared. 'That's strange! It's red, orange, yellow . . .'

Aidan continued, 'Green, er, blue, indigo, violet. What's strange?'

'Hannah's right,' said Olly. 'There's another colour in there, but I can't quite make it out. The rainbow keeps shimmering. It's . . . it's gold!'

Hannah's eyes twinkled. 'Maybe there's a pot of gold at the end of the rainbow!'

'That could be another adventure on Magic Farm,' said Aidan. 'But for now, I suppose we better go back home. Our mums and dads will be wondering where we are.'

Olly went to say goodbye to Star. She nuzzled him, tickling his ear. 'We're going now,' he said, 'but we'll come and see you again soon.'

'I hope so,' said a voice behind him. It was Patch, with Muck, Tishoo and

Sunny. 'Magic Farm wouldn't be the same without you three visiting us.'

'And helping,' said Tishoo. 'Ha-ha-hat-tishoo!' His hat landed on a very surprised Star's head.

The four Hayseeds walked with the children to the magic scarecrow. The air was fresh after the rain, and filled with the scent of wild flowers.

Olly watched Aidan spin the scarecrow and disappear, then it was Hannah's turn. She waved goodbye, whirled round and vanished.

'Bye, Hayseeds,' said Olly, taking hold of the scarecrow's arm. He whooshed round into a silvery spin,

then tumbled on to the grass of Golden Valley.

The three friends began the walk home, chatting about the day.

'I really love Magic Farm, don't you?' Hannah said.

'It's all right, I suppose,' Aidan said, before bursting out laughing. 'Only joking. It's the best!'

Olly was quieter than them. He was remembering the thrill of leaping from the tree on to Star's back. *I'll be happy around* all *of our animals now*, he thought, *like a real farmer should be*.

As they reached the top of the hill and started down the other side towards Golden Valley Farm, Olly saw Toffee grazing in her field.

He broke into a run towards the pony. 'I can't wait for tomorrow,' he cried. 'I'm going riding again!

Yippeeee!' He leant over the fence and held out his hand so that Toffee drew near and nuzzled her nose in his palm. It was soft as velvet and tickly. She raised her head, blowing air out

of her nostrils, almost as if she was as excited as Olly to go riding tomorrow.

It had been the perfect day with a magical zebra, and tomorrow would be another amazing day with the best pony in the world.

'I'm so happy I could burst,' Olly told Toffee. The little pony neighed in agreement.

EGMONT PRESS: ETHICAL PUBLISHING

Egmont Press is about turning writers into successful authors and children into passionate readers – producing books that enrich and entertain. As a responsible children's publisher, we go even further, considering the world in which our consumers are growing up.

Safety First
Naturally, all of our books meet legal safety requirements. But we go further than this; every book with play value is tested to the highest standards – if it fails, it's back to the drawing-board.

Made Fairly
We are working to ensure that the workers involved in our supply chain – the people that make our books – are treated with fairness and respect.

Responsible Forestry
We are committed to ensuring all our papers come from environmentally and socially responsible forest sources.

For more information, please visit our website at
www.egmont.co.uk/ethicalpublishing